DONUT THE DRAGON

Written by **Greg Wachs**   Illustrated by **Eugene Blissful**
Published by **Funky Dreamer Storytime**

Donut the Dragon
© 2017 Greg Wachs, Funky Dreamer Storytime

Adapted from the original podcast entitled
"Donut the Dragon" by **Greg Wachs**
Podcast story and original music
by **Greg Wachs** © 2017

Donut the Dragon is wholly owned by **Greg Wachs**

Written by **Greg Wachs**

Illustrated by **Eugene Blissful**

Donut the Dragon is available on
www.funkydreamerstorytime.com

Printed in the United States of America

First Printing, 2017

ISBN-13: 978-1545125434

Published by **Funky Dreamer Storytime**

Funky Dreamer Storytime
Greg Wachs
139 North Laurel Ave.
Los Angeles, CA 90048
www.funkydreamerstorytime.com
310-966-7536
greg@funkydreamerstorytime.com
mediacom2020@gmail.com

twitter: **@podcasts4kids**

Eugene Blissful
eugene.stepanenko@gmail.com
eugeneblissful.tumblr.com
instagram.com/eugene_blissful

Ordering Information
Special discounts are available on quantity purchases
by corporations, education, K–12, and associations.
For details, contact the publisher at the info above.
Orders by bookstores and wholesalers, please contact
us at the info above.

Dedication

*This book is dedicated to my wife, Shula,
and my daughter, Anabelle Rae, who have both
helped me write the best story ever, our life together.
(And, I'm glad this one is not a dream!)*

- Greg Wachs

To all my family and friends, I hope you enjoy this story.

- Eugene Blissful

yle jumped out of the airplane, goggles on, parachute backpack, and an incredible feeling of pride. *Not bad for a ten-year-old,* he thought.

Falling through the blue sky, slightly cloudy, no chance of rain, wind on his face, heart pounding. **"Wow,"** he said out loud.

The view was amazing—the four lakes below, the forest off to the right, the mountains in the distance, and all the houses scattered all over Tillendale.

He started counting swimming pools. "One, two, three...Wait a minute, what am I doing? Okay, remember the training, remember the rules, stay calm, don't panic." He checked his watch. "Right on track...three...two...ONE," he shouted. **"Yippeeeee!"** and he pulled the cord. Nothing. He gave it another yank. Still nothing. He pulled it with all his might, and it snapped off in his hand.

"Okay, stay calm, remember the training...Backup parachute. Yes." Yank. Nothing.

His heart stopped, he held his breath, his mind swirled...everything started to go black. And then he looked down. All black. Then the black moved. The black swooped. The black did a U-turn, and suddenly a huge black dragon with deep yellow eyes was staring at him, three feet from his face.

Okay, I must be dreaming, Kyle thought. *Or maybe I'm already dead. Yeah, that's it. I fell to the earth, and I'm lying there, and this is my I-just-died final dream.*

"Need some help?"

asked the dragon.

Kyle stared at him, frozen.

"I can save you, but we just need to make a little deal first," said the dragon. "I save you, and you buy me twelve donuts."

Kyle stared at him, frozen.

"Of course you should say yes and agree to the deal 'cause, you know, you're like, falling. And I'm falling with you, but the thing is, I have wings—really cool big black wings—and you just have, like, little human arms, which are not really so good for flying. Know what I mean?"

Kyle stared, frozen.

"Oh, how rude of me. I haven't had a chance to make a formal introduction. Please allow me to introduce myself..."

"They call me Dragor the dragon. Some people call me Donut 'cause I like donuts so much. Yes, Dragor, and what's more, I open doors, for the ladies. Yes, I am a gentleman. I'm polite, I sleep during the day, and I fly around at night."

"I've got a huge appetite, but I also have a great big heart. I save people, I shop at Kmart, I wine and dine my neighbors, I strive to be a savior, and I savor cookies and tea. I do yoga, I eat frozen yogurt 'cause it's good for me, I fly upside down, yeah, I show off a little. I like M&Ms, Milky Ways, I also like Skittles, But I also eat carrot sticks, broccoli, and edamame."

"And hey, you should also know, I really love my mommy. My dad is cool, too. He taught me how to swim in the pool and in the ocean. I'm smaller than a blue whale, but sharks are afraid. (Imagine that notion!) One human designed a cage for me, but I ain't mad at him."

"You can't catch a dragon—not Dragor!"

"I'll fly, skip, and hop. You'll find me at the donut shop. Un me saw, sibbido ma, batamoso swayna memodo se seka moo. You see when I eat all those donuts, what they make me do? I like the jelly donuts and the chocolate covered donuts, the old-fashioned donuts, and the rainbow sprinkles, too. Then I go home and sleep all day. If you ate that many donuts, wouldn't you?"

"Then I fly around at night, only landing when I'm ready for my next delicious bite. Yeah, you can find me at the donut shop, alright? And I don't stop."

"My name is Drag— My name— My name is Dragor."

Kyle stared at him, frozen.

"Listen, kid, I know you're scared right now, and I get that, but do me a favor. If we have a deal, just blink your eyes."

Kyle blinked.

The dragon swooped underneath Kyle. His back felt warm and leathery.

"Show me where to land," the dragon said, looking back at Kyle. Kyle pointed to the football field near his house. The dragon dipped his wing, and they glided downward.

Safe on the ground, Kyle climbed off and started slowly walking towards his house, head down, in shock, like a zombie.

"Hello?" said the dragon. Kyle kept walking. **WHOOOOOOSH!**

Hot flames shot past Kyle's head!

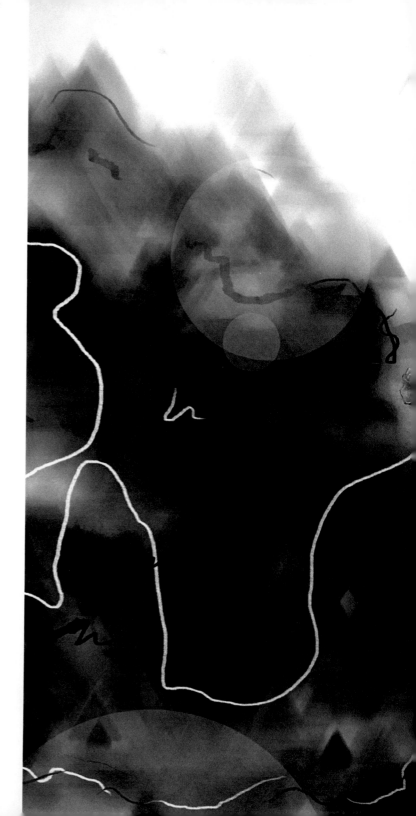

He spun around
and fell on his butt,
looking up at the dragon,
squinting, the sun in
his eyes.

**"Where are my
twelve donuts?"**
asked the dragon, taking
a step towards Kyle.

Kyle reached into
his pocket, pulled
out two dollars,
and held it up.

"That's enough for
about four donuts,"
said the dragon.
"We agreed to
twelve."

Bounce, bounce, bounce. A soccer ball flew off the football field, rolled across the street, and stopped at Kyle's feet. Kyle's friend Jason ran up, out of breath. Then he stooped down and picked up the ball. Then his eyes moved slowly from Kyle's feet, up his legs, and to his face. "Hey, Kyle, wanna come kick the ball around?"

Kyle just stared at him.

"You okay, man? You look like you seen a ghost."

Kyle nodded towards the dragon. "What?" asked Jason.

"Dragon," said Kyle softly.

"Dragon?" asked Jason. "What about a dragon?"

Jason can't see the dragon! Kyle thought to himself. Then he remembered—Jason and his family moved to Korea six months ago.

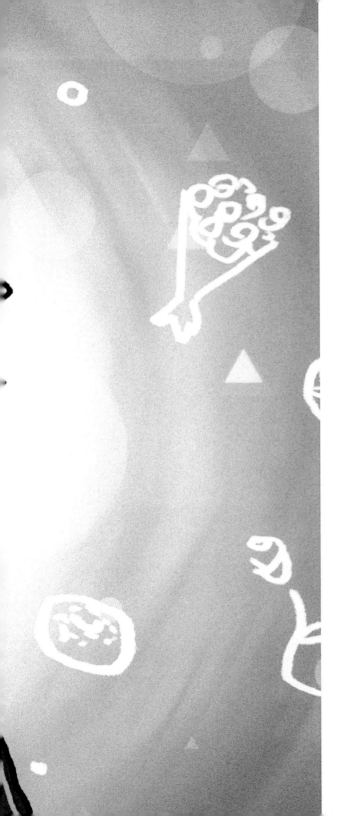

This IS a dream, Kyle thought to himself. ***I KNEW IT!***

The dragon snorted black smoke. Kyle could smell it, and he could feel the heat. He closed his eyes and concentrated.

"What are you doing?" asked the dragon.

"What are you doing?" asked Jason.

Kyle focused all of his energy on one thought, and **POOF!**

A beautiful girl dragon appeared. DARK BLUE, with sky blue outlines along her wings, a red crown with black ribbons hanging down, and a diamond right between her eyes.

"Wow," said the dragon.

"Okay, mister," she said to the dragon, "you'd better forget about that donut shop and start moving towards the flower shop."

Kyle watched as they held wings and flew off towards the clouds.

Then Kyle woke up,
falling through the sky!
He had fainted after his
first chute didn't open.
"I KNEW IT!"
he said.
"This was all a dream!
Stay calm, don't panic."

He checked his watch. Three...two...one...
he pulled the backup cord.
WHOOSH!
The chute opened, and
he began drifting slowly down
to the football field.

His feet hit the ground,
and he rolled onto the grass,
then kneeled on one knee
as the parachute slowly
crumpled beside him.

Then he looked up towards the sky
just in time to see two black dots
disappear into the clouds.

He looked at his watch.
Time for dinner,
he thought, and he unclipped
the safety belt.
"Hey, Kyle."
He looked up. It was Jason.
  "Jason? I thought you moved
  to Korea."
  "Yeah, we're just back in town
  visiting my grandparents for
  the holidays."

Kyle stood up and swung the pack over his shoulder.

"Cool. Well, I have two bucks. Wanna get some donuts?"

"Sure," said Jason, and they walked towards the donut shop.

Kyle glanced back over his shoulder towards the sky. Then with a little smile, Kyle blinked.

About the Author

Greg Wachs is a kids' book author, kids' podcast creator, musician, and father living in West Hollywood, CA, with his wife, Shula, and daughter, Anabelle Rae.

About the Illustrator

Eugene Blissful is a freelance artist with many interests and side projects. He lives in St. Petersburg and Milan, has studied art at St. Petersburg State University, and is now a student at the St. Petersburg Institute of Theology and Philosophy. He enjoys traveling, playing his viola da gamba, and reading books on history and cultural studies.

Enjoy all of the books
by
Greg Wachs

  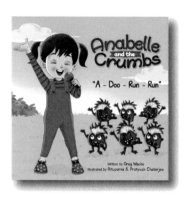

Remember Kids these are, **"Pod-Books"**, which means they have a matching podcast!
Just go to www.funkydreamerstorytime.com or search iTunes for the name of the book.
Each podcast reads you the book. They are also chock full of really cool music!
So, fire up a podcast, then kick back, and enjoy the adventure!

59505714R00020

Made in the USA
San Bernardino, CA
04 December 2017